I0684174

A Case of Mistaken Identity

EO Writes

For information, address:
EO Writes
lizzy@eowrites.com

EO Writes created the cover and interior design.

A Case of Mistaken Identity/ EO Writes, First Edition.
ISBN:979-8-9904599-2-2

Published 2024. Printed in the United States of America.

A Little Peek

Should you wish to explore my published articles on homeschooling, they are available for reading here: https://eowrites.com/homeschooling/

Access the bonus material "A Case of Mistaken Identity" Activity book by going here.

To explore my website, simply click on this link: https://eowrites.com/.

Contents

Proloque

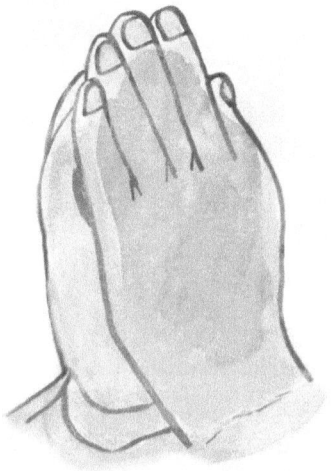

Pray without ceasing.

Lady Wisdom: Sadie, why the sigh? What's wrong?

Sadie handed Lady Wisdom an envelope, which she opened: This arrived in yesterday's mail.

Lady Wisdom: A Subpoena?

Sadie: Yes, I received a summons to appear in court regarding my purpose.

Lady Wisdom: God is in control! He won't let you down. I have a verse for you.
"What shall we then say to these things? If God be for us, who can be against us?" Romans 8:31

Sadie: Wow, Lady Wisdom, thank you for sharing such a great verse. I'll do my best to keep that in mind.

Lady Wisdom: You are welcome, Sadie. I'm sorry to end our visit early today, but they need me downtown. You know me helping people brings me great joy. Goodbye for now. Don't forget to hold the verse close to your heart and read it often throughout the day."

Sadie, while getting ready for bed, and feeling this deep plummet feeling in her spirit, said to herself: What if I am denied my purpose?

Fear entered her bedroom and said: Your life will be filled with longing for the unattainable.

Sadie turned around with an authoritative voice: "Fear, get out!"

Fear broke into laughter: Okay, but you know I'm always here if you want to talk about the past.

Sadie, to herself: Okay, pull yourself together, girl. God has already promised you that your calling is a sure thing.

"What time, I am afraid. I will trust in thee." Psalm 56:3.

Father, I'm filled with a deep sense of dread as I anticipate going to court. Help me keep my focus on You. What was that verse Lady Wisdom gave me again? Hmm. Oh, yeah. "What shall we then say to these things? If God be for us, who can be against us?" Romans 8:31 Thank you, Father, for the reminder."

Sadie, answering her ringing phone: Oh, hi Lady Wisdom.

Lady Wisdom: Hi Sadie. How are you doing?
Sadie: I'm doing okay. Thank you for asking.

Lady Wisdom: No problem. Lady Prudence will pick you up in the morning for the courthouse.

Sadie: Thank you.

Lady Wisdom: You are welcome. Goodbye.

Sadie: Goodbye.

The next morning

Lady Prudence, greeting Sadie as she opened her door: Good morning, Sadie!

Sadie: Good morning, Lady Prudence. It sure is a beautiful day.

Lady Prudence: Yes, it is! How was your sleep?

Sadie, looking with glowing eyes at Lady Prudence: It was good.

Lady Prudence: Before you went to sleep, did you check out the verse Lady Wisdom gave you?

Sadie proclaimed: Yes, I did!

Lady Prudence, with a big grin, looked deep into her eyes while holding her hands: Trust that things will work out because God is in charge. Let's make sure we get you to the courthouse a few minutes early.

God has already promised you that your calling is a sure thing.

Chapter 1

Transition

Proverbs 3:16

Lady Prudence: There's the courthouse. Remember, God is with you.

As Sadie approached the building, its elegance overwhelmed her. The elaborate pillars showed its age. Inside, it was even more impressive than its exterior. In the corridor, there were endless doors and a black stone flooring. As they walked through the hallway together to the courtroom Sadie turned to Lady Prudence.
Sadie: I've lived here for years and yet never noticed this building.
The tension in the hallway was great. As Sadie entered the courtroom, she was in awe of her surroundings. The floor was a brown tile with a lining of gold. A black sparkle resembling stars adorned the ceiling.
The room reminded her of the ballroom scene in Beauty and the Beast.
Clerk: All rise. Court is now in session. Honorable Judge Justice is presiding.

Judge: Thank you, please take your seat. We call the Case of Mistaken Identity now in session. Is the Plaintiff ready?

Plaintiff: Yes, Your Honor.

Judge: Is the Defense ready?

Defense: I am, Your Honor.

Judge: We will now hear open statements from the defense.

Defense: Thank you, Your Honor. My name is Sadie. I will represent myself in this case. God does not consult our past or those from our past when he calls us forth. God's purpose for me is a sure thing, for it was decided at the beginning of time. I am asking for a verdict of not guilty not on my merits but on His!

Judge: We will now hear open statements from the Plaintiff.

Plaintiff, with great pride: Thank you, Your Honor. My name is Condemnation. Today, you will hear Sadie's story.

Her life so far makes us think she is not suitable for God's purpose. We are requesting a guilty verdict.

Judge: Thank you, counsel. Defendant, call your first witness.

Defendant: Your Honor I would like to call Lady Wisdom and Lady Prudence to the stand.

Judge: Lady Wisdom and Lady Prudence, please take the stand. Before you sit, can you both please raise your right hand? Do you promise to tell the whole truth, nothing but the truth, so help you, God?

Lady Wisdom and Lady Prudence in unison: We do!

Judge: You may take your seats.

Defendant: Tell the court what your relationship is with the young lady.

Lady Wisdom: Where should I start?

Defendant: How about at five?

Lady Wisdom: I think I will start with the first day of kindergarten. I looked at the clock, surprised at the time. I didn't want to miss her big day. I hurried down the street to the school through the crowds of children heading to their classrooms. I spotted her and went over to talk to her. She greeted me with a twirl and a giggle. I visited with her until her teacher came in. She was excited. Of course, I was concerned about her education. The focus was on man, not God. It's such an odd thing to me to designate a building for teaching young people, yet they leave out wisdom, true wisdom. How does one find their way without knowing good and evil? As the years went by, going to school became hostile. Her classmates picked on her and she would do her best to not let it bother her, but I could tell it was having its toll on her. She didn't understand why her classmates didn't like her.

I shared a verse with her that was her constant companion through grade school -… "but I say unto you, that ye resist not evil: but whosoever shall smite thee on thy right cheek, turn to him the other cheek." Matthew 5:39.

Defendant: Lady Wisdom, did you ever visit her at her house? What was her childhood home like?

Lady Wisdom: I visited her often at her house. She sat in her playroom for many hours surrounded by small wooden people and a village of Fisher Price buildings: a farm, a school, a hospital, etc. She looked like a young queen ruling her vast kingdom!

Other times I would come over to visit, and she would invite me to her bedroom, where we would listen to stories about castles, princesses, and dragons. These particular stories had her on the edge of her seat. You could see from her dreamy eyes that she loved these stories the most. I would often remind her that man cannot meet your every need. Only God can. She would look at me with a big smile. She had such a respondent heart.

My favorite visits with her were when she would attend church. Her parents were adamant about the family attending church. We would sit together, and she would glow as the Word of God was being taught. The teachers taught the Sunday school lessons using pieces of felt. She loved the vibrant colors and how the stories came to life on the storyboard. Sometimes, she would volunteer to help the teacher with the pieces.

One time at Vacation Bible School, her eyes lit up when the Pastor mentioned that those who memorized the most verses in their age group would receive a Bible. She was determined from that moment to win that Bible. Every day for two weeks, she recited the verse of the day to her teacher. By the end of the two weeks, she had that Bible.
I jumped up in the air and gave her a high-five! I told her to hide God's word in her heart like treasure, it will be there when you need it!

Lady Prudence was her best cheerleader…

Lady Prudence: Yes, I was!

Lady Wisdom: She encouraged her every step of the way, reminding her of why it was so important to memorize the scriptures.

Lady Prudence: I would tell her often, "Hide it in your heart, girl. It will help you know the difference between good and evil."

Lady Wisdom: Oh, I don't want to forget camp. She attended camp three summers in a row. She would talk about it for hours. They served breakfast in the big cafeteria, and if you were lucky, they would call you up to receive a letter from home. Games and chapel at night. I loved listening to her sing with her new camp friends. She listened to the message that was given, and every year she would rededicate her life to Jesus. Every year, they brought out a board at the end of the week. If you gave your heart to Jesus or rededicated your life, you had to sign it. "They have overcome by the blood of the lamb, and the word of their testimony." Revelations 12:11.

Lady Prudence: Your Honor. Can I add something?

Judge: Go ahead, Lady Prudence.

Lady Prudence: She also attended Church School, which I know she enjoyed, but had a hard time leaving the public school to catch the bus to go to Church School because of a conflict of interest, for Fridays were movie day.

Judge: Thank you, Lady Prudence. You may continue, Lady Wisdom.

Lady Wisdom: I was thrilled that she actively took part in activities that taught her the Bible, but as the years went by, I could see from her changing demeanor that she was not prioritizing time for reading her Bible. Only by reading the Bible can we learn God's ways. The Bible is a guide to right living.

I tried to talk to her about it, but she would shrug me off and go on her merry way to do something she deemed more exciting.

I caught her one time talking out loud, as though rehearsing a line for a play, a damsel in distress and her Prince coming to take her away. She was daydreaming again. Not surprising with all that she was dealing with.

One time, while at the mall, I noticed some new friends competing for her attention. She was curious and her curiosity was pulling her in their direction. Now and then I would catch her looking their way. I would get her attention once again. However, I was noticing her attention span towards me and the things of God were shortening.

Defendant: What was she dealing with at home?

Lady Wisdom: Her oldest brother had a health condition. He required a lot of time and energy from her parents. No fault of theirs. The stress of the situation was affecting the entire house.

Defendant: When did you see a change in her demeanor?

Lady Wisdom: I would say in sixth grade. That's when I started seeing her pulling away from God. Then there was the transition from grade school to high school. Of course, Lady Prudence and I were at her sixth-grade graduation! Not to mention it's a celebration and we so love being around people. We walked in and sat close to where she was. Our presence wasn't welcomed, but we were there for her.

The past year was a hard one for her. She had lost a dear friend to cancer. The sight of the new school building, tall and overshadowing the smaller one, troubled her. Darkness encroached upon her face. "I'm not ready!," she would say. I gave her a grin and said, "If you ever need anything, I am here." Yes, I have to admit to you she wasn't ready.

Judge: Lady Prudence, did you have something to add?

Lady Prudence: Yes, I do, thank you. I knew the transition to the high school would be her hardest years. She is a fighter! She has been through a lot and yet here she is!

Defendant: Lady Prudence, why did you feel that the transition to high school would be the hardest years for her?

Lady Prudence: She had not discovered her story yet, her place where she fit. Peer pressure is the strongest in the adolescent years.

Defendant: Thank you, Lady Prudence. Lady Wisdom, what are your thoughts on the education she received? Was it a good fit?

Lady Wisdom: When I look back over her grade school years, I think to myself, "If only her parents would have chosen homeschooling." Sunday mornings are not enough when these young people are sitting in that building eight hours a day, five days a week, receiving head knowledge, not heart knowledge. The Word of God is alive and ever speaking, whereas the knowledge of this world is just dusty old books that are forgotten.

Defendant: Lady Wisdom, you said you noticed she was distancing herself from God in sixth grade. Was there a point where she pulled away from you and, if so, when was that?

Lady Wisdom: Her gaze was not as bright as it was, as sadness filled her eyes that Summer after 6th grade graduation. Summer came, and I reached out to her weekly, but she was not interested. I let her know I was here if she needed to talk. Sundays brought me such joy, for I knew I would see her. One Sunday she came in and I noticed this one boy was getting her attention. His charm distracted her from listening to the message, which was unlike her. When I approached her about it, her eyes darkened. I don't need you. Leave me alone! Sadly, Lady Prudence and I turned and headed for the door.

Lady Prudence: Your Honor, can I bring something to the court's attention?

Judge: Proceed.

Lady Prudence: She grew up with fairy tales. They had a major impression on her childlike heart. The dangers with stories like Cinderella and Snow White are they give the false impression that all you need is a man. With the story *Snow White*, it was a Prince that brought her back to life. In Cinderella, an encounter at a royal ball led her to wedding bells and freedom from her wicked family. In both stories, they went from rags to riches because of a man. The one I do, however, find intriguing is the *Beauty and the Beast*. I will save that for another time.
My point is we can only find true happiness in God. Young hearts are so impressionable. I would like to add, as she came of age, her father withdrew somewhat from her, for he thought it was more the mother's role to mold her into a promising young lady.

Judge: Would the Plaintiff like to cross?

Plaintiff: Yes, I would, Your Honor.

Judge: Very well, then proceed.

Plaintiff: Lady Wisdom, are any of those new friends you mentioned present in this courtroom?

Lady Wisdom: Yes. Madame Folly.
Plaintiff: Thank you, Lady Wisdom.

Judge: You may sit down, ladies.

"Thy word have I hid in mine heart,
that I might not sin against thee."
Psalm 119:11

Chapter 2

Impressions

Proverbs 5:5

Judge: Plaintiff, call your first witness.

Plaintiff: Your Honor I would like to call Madame Folly to the stand.

Judge: Madame Folly, please take the stand. Before you sit, can you please raise your right hand? Do you promise to tell the whole truth, nothing but the truth, so help you, God?

Madame Folly: Hmph…

Judge: A yes would be sufficient.

Madame Folly: Yes.

Judge: You may take your seat.

Plaintiff: Tell the court about your relationship with this young lady.

Madam Folly, with a mischievous look: Age eighteen, that's a great place to start.

Judge: No fifteen will suffice.

Madame Folly: Fine. Ugh… She was a good little church girl. I knew she would get bored and call me. I have always been around, but when she was fifteen, I was her best friend. I am a lot more fun than Lady Wisdom and Lady Prudence. That summer, she attended a party and met this guy. The two took a liking to each other.

Judge: Would the Defendant like to cross?

Defendant: Yes, Your Honor. Madame Folly, how old was the guy?

Madame Folly: That's irrelevant.

Judge: Just answer the question.

Defendant: He was nineteen, correct?

Madame Folly: Yeah, what of it?

Defendant: She shot back, "In my defense, I was a child. He was a man. I know it doesn't excuse my actions. I'm just saying I was young. "When I was a child, I spoke and thought and reasoned as a child. But when I grew up, I put away childish things."

I Corinthians 13:11 (NLT)

Defendant: I rest.

Plaintiff: Madame Folly, what happened after they met?

Madame Folly: They exchanged numbers, dated for three years, then went on their merry way, end of the story.

Judge: Wait a minute. There are details that need to be examined. You may take your seat, Madame Folly. Does the defense have a witness they would like to call to the stand?

Defendant: Yes, Your Honor. I call Lady Prudence to the stand.
Judge: Lady Prudence, please take the stand.

Defendant: Lady Prudence, did you see any changes in the young lady after she started dating this gentleman?

Lady Prudence: Yes, I did. At first it was subtle, then it progressed.

Defendant: In what ways? Please explain.

Lady Prudence: Her taste in music, the way she presented herself.

She was defiant to her parents, and did not desire the things of God.It was as though she was dealing with a case of mistaken identity. Pardon the pun. This was not who she was at all. She was a child of God who lost her way.

Defendant: Do you feel this gentleman had a profound impression on her at such a young age?

Lady Prudence stared into the Judge's eyes: Yes, I do. Judge, can I remind the court of a truth?

Judge: Go ahead.

Lady Prudence: "Do not be misled: Bad company corrupts good character." I Corinthians 15:33 (NIV)

Judge: Thank you, Lady Prudence, for sharing that truth.

Madame Folly shrugged her shoulders and rolled her eyes while letting out a deep sigh...

Judge: Plaintiff, do you want to cross?

Plaintiff: I rest.

Judge: You may step down, Lady Prudence. Does the Defendant have a witness they would like to call to the stand?

Defendant: Your Honor, I would like to call Lady Wisdom to the stand.
Judge: Lady Wisdom, please take the stand.

Madame Folly jumped up from her seat, demanded to be heard: Wait a minute! She wasn't hanging around her as much as I was!

Judge: Madame Folly, please be silent and sit down. You are not on the stand.

Judge: Lady Wisdom, you may proceed.

Defendant: Lady Wisdom, please tell this court what you saw during this time.

Lady Wisdom: I saw a lot of turmoil in her soul. She asked me to accompany her to counseling. She was dealing with a lot in her life. The bullying was escalating, her best friend was the aforementioned gentlemen, and she felt abandoned by her parents who did not understand what she was going through. She was out of character and in a dreary place. I tried to talk to her, but she was not listening. But she did, however, want me by her side when she would see her counselor.

Defendant: Thank you, Lady Wisdom.

Judge: Plaintiff, do you want to cross?

Plaintiff: Yes, Your Honor. So, Lady Wisdom, she was a bit of a troublemaker, with no respect for authority?

Lady Wisdom: Yes, she was. The word is 'was.' She lost her way.

Plaintiff: I rest, Your Honor.

Judge: Defendant, do you have more questions for Lady Wisdom?

Defendant: The defense rests.

Judge: Lady Wisdom, you may take your seat.

Judge: Does the Defendant have a witness they would like to call to the stand?

Defendant: Your Honor, I would like to call Encourager to the stand.

Judge: Encourager, please take the stand. Before you sit, can you please raise your right hand? Do you promise to tell the whole truth, nothing but the truth, so help you, God?

Encourager: Yes, I do, Your Honor.

Judge: You may take your seat.

Defendant: Encourager, when the young lady was twelve, her sister sang a song at their church titled *Is There an Orphan in Your Home* by Connie Scott. Is that correct?

Madame Folly defiantly stood up and loudly exclaimed: No, no, no! Why are we going back there? That was back when she was twelve, this is supposed to be about when she's fifteen?

Judge: Madame Folly, please be quiet.

Madame Folly scowled at the Judge: Really?

Judge: Madame Folly, I will have respect in my courtroom. If you continue with these outbursts of disrespect towards her story, I will have you removed. Is that understood?

Madame Folly: Loud and clear.

Defendant: Encourager, please tell the court about that day.

Encourager: She was sitting with her parents. As her sister sang *Is There an Orphan in Your Home*, I noticed she was fidgeting, trying to keep her composure. She got up and asked me to accompany her. Her legs quivered uncontrollably as she struggled to maintain balance in her towering high heels.

After the song, her sister came into the bathroom. She cried and hugged her, and they talked for a while. Then they both went back into the sanctuary and sat down. I noticed by the expression on her parents' face that they were not happy with her abrupt walk out. They seemed embarrassed. Her response to that song meant something was wrong at home.

Defendant: Thank you, Encourager.

Judge: Plaintiff, do you want to cross?

Plaintiff: No, Your Honor, I rest.

Judge: Encourager, you may step down.

Judge: Does the Defendant have a witness they would like to call to the stand?

Defendant: Your Honor, I would like to call Lady Wisdom back to the stand.

Judge: Lady Wisdom, please take the stand.

Defendant: Lady Wisdom, can you explain to the courts the definition of "orphan"?

Lady Wisdom: The kids definition of an orphan by Webster is
1. a child whose parents have died.
2. one who has had protection or advantage taken away.

Defendant: Thank you, Lady Wisdom.

Judge: Plaintiff, do you want to cross?

Plaintiff, looking rather proud of himself, he turned around and looked at those in the courtroom: Yes, I do, Your Honor. Lady Wisdom, thank you for sharing the definition of an orphan, but I cannot see how this fits in this case. Both parents are alive. She has a roof over her head, she's well taken care of. Please explain.

Lady Wisdom: Someone can experience loneliness even in a room full of people, just like in this situation where she had parents, but there had been a disconnection with them for some time. There was a communication problem. In her heart, she felt like an orphan, alone and misunderstood.

Plaintiff: Thank you, Lady Wisdom.

Judge: Lady Wisdom, you may step down.

Judge: Does the Defendant have a witness they would like to call to the stand?

Defendant: Your Honor I would like to call the Encourager back to the stand.

Judge: Encourager, please take the stand.

Defendant: Encourager, can you share with the court any other times you witnessed something like that? An act of kindness that left an impression on the young lady?

Encourager: Yes, I can. The church had a Secret Pal ministry, in which an adult chose a child in the church to anonymously bless. One day, she came in to find a gift addressed to her on the table. I know it meant a lot to her. Ladies and gentlemen, to this day, she still has it. It's ratted and torn but still means a lot to her. This proves that acts of kindness make a difference.

Defendant: Thank you, Encourager.

Judge: Plaintiff, do you want to cross?

Plaintiff: I rest.

Judge: Encourager, you may step down.

Judge: We are going to take a lunch break. We will meet back here in 50 minutes.

Lady Prudence: Judge, may I give some evidence to the Clerk before we go on lunch break?

Judge: Yes, you may, Lady Prudence.

Lady Prudence hands a slip of paper to the Clerk.

"The LORD is nigh unto them that are of a broken heart; and saveth such as be of a contrite spirit." Psalm 34:18.

In the hallway

Lady Prudence: Sadie, how are you holding up?

The Defendant turned and looked at her with downcast eyes: Hearing this part of my story is hard. There are things in my teen years I am not proud of. I was so foolish then.

Lady Prudence embraced her and whispered in her ear: That was then, this is now. It's going to be alright, remember God is in control.

Madame Folly, with an evil smirk, walked over to the Plaintiff and whispered into his ear: Condemnation, what are we going to do? This case is not moving in our favor?

Condemnation: Do you have anything?

Madame Folly, sporting an evil grin while looking at Sadie: I think I do. Everyone started making their way back into the courtroom as Madame Folly went to her car.

Inside the courtroom

Clerk: All rise. Court is in session. The Honorable Judge Justice is presiding. We call the Case of Mistaken Identity now in session.

Judge: Thank you, you may take your seat. Does the Defendant have a witness they would like to call to the stand?

Defendant: Yes, Your Honor. I call Broken to the stand.

Judge: Broken, please take the stand. Before you sit, can you please raise your right hand? Do you promise to tell the whole truth, nothing but the truth, so help you, God?

Broken: Yes.

Judge: You may be seated.

Defendant: Broken, how did you come to know the young lady?
Broken: I have been around her for a long time. She has gone through many hard seasons. What is it you want me to share?

Defendant: Broken, please tell the court about the breakup with the aforementioned gentlemen.

Broken: Well, uh…

Judge: Madame Folly, you are late.

Madame Folly: Sorry, something came to my attention.

She slips a note to the Plaintiff and whispers, "This will be her undoing."

Romans 8:1 "No condemnation for those who walk in the spirit, *not the flesh.*" (Emphasis)

Judge: Proceed, Broken.

Broken: He called her and said he needed time to think, and they parted ways.

Defendant: How did the young lady take it?

Broken: Not well at all.

Defendant: Please elaborate.

Broken: Ladies and gentlemen, she would sit on her porch night after night. Watching, waiting, looking for him. She was quite distraught, hoping he would come around again. Their hearts were one and now there was a severe break. She was beside herself. I've never seen her so lost as she was.

Defendant: Thank you, Broken.

Judge: Plaintiff, do you want to cross?

Plaintiff: I rest.

Judge: Thank you, Broken. You may step down.

Plaintiff: I call Lady Prudence to the stand.

Judge: Lady Prudence, please take the stand.

Plaintiff: Please elaborate to the court what she was going through.

Lady Prudence: She confided in me. She believed with all her heart that he loved her. She mentioned marriage to him. It was not long after that they parted ways. She was still very much connected to him. The two had become one in every sense of the word. Yes, as Broken had said, she sat on that porch at night for some time looking for him. The same porch on which she sat nestled in her father's arms as a small child. But now she sat alone. She dealt with this grief alone.

Plaintiff: Thank you, Lady Prudence.

Judge: Defendant, do you want to cross?

Defendant: Yes, I do, Your Honor. Did she get closure?

Lady Prudence: No, she did not. It was her senior year of high school, the year she wore black. She was sporting her grieving heart on the outside. She was indeed in mourning.

Defendant: Thank you, Lady Prudence.

Judge: Plaintiff, do you want to cross?

Plaintiff: Yes, I do.

Plaintiff: Lady Prudence, did she not violate God's standards by sleeping with him? Is that not forbidden, to be saved for marriage?

Lady Prudence: Yes, she did, but may I remind the court she was young. When she was twenty-three, she came back to Jesus. I would also like to add a truth - "for all have sinned and come short of the glory of God." Romans 3:23,24

Plaintiff: That is all, thank you, Lady Prudence.

Judge: Lady Prudence, you may step down.

Judge: Does the Defendant have a witness they would like to call to the stand?

Defendant: Your Honor, I would like to call Fear to the stand.

Judge: Fear, please take the stand. Before you sit, can you please raise your right hand? Do you promise to tell the whole truth, nothing but the truth, so help you, God?

Fear: Uh…yes. I think so.

Judge: You may be seated.

Defendant: How well did you know the young lady?

Fear, with sweat clinging to his brow and his eyes dropping their gaze to the rug underneath his feet: I knew her, really… Well, uh, maybe I shouldn't talk about her. I might get in trouble. Uh… sorry.

Defendant: Stay with me Fear. How well did you know this young lady?
Fear: I knew her well enough.

Defendant: When she was twenty-three, there was a major turning point. Could you tell the court about her brother's death and how it affected her?

Fear, with a face absent of color, he stuttered the words out: Her brother died when she was twenty-three. We met up at the funeral. It was then that she faced her own mortality. When I say fearful, I mean it. She didn't sleep well or eat well. I was her best friend for quite a long season. We hung out together day and night until she met that one girl who ruined everything!

Defendant: Have you ever met up again with her? Can you elaborate on that?

Fear tightly grips the chair's arms, his gaze fixed on the judge: I have always been in her life. But when her brother died, she welcomed me as her best friend.

Judge: Plaintiff, do you want to cross?

Plaintiff: I rest.

Fear: Am I going to get in trouble for sharing? I uh..don't want any trouble.

Judge: Fear, you may step down. Does the Plaintiff have a witness they would like to call to the stand?

Plaintiff: Your Honor, I would like to call Lady Wisdom back to the stand.

Judge: Lady Wisdom, please take the stand.

Plaintiff: Lady Wisdom, is not fear the opposite of faith?

Lady Wisdom: Yes, it is!

Plaintiff: She's a child of God, is she not? Yet she dealt with consuming fear? Explain.

Lady Wisdom: Everyone deals with fear. However, in this case, she was not right with God, and she knew it.

"There is no fear in love, but perfect love casteth out fear: because fear has torment. He that feareth is not made perfect in love." I John 4:18

Plaintiff: That's all. Thank you, Lady Wisdom.

Judge: Defendant, do you have questions for Lady Wisdom?

Defendant: Yes, I do, Your Honor. Could you tell the court about the girl she met online?

Madame Folly rises, stares at the judge, and asks about the time from eighteen to twenty-three: I had such a blast during that time. This is ridiculous. I have so much to say, but I am not being given the stand.

Judge: You are out of order, Madame Folly.

Madame Folly: How about the time when she…

The judge stood up angrily, looking Madame Folly in the eye, and warned: I will have you escorted out if you say one more word.

Madame Folly: She deserves nothing good. She is bad to the bone. Give me the stand and I will spill it all.

Judge: I have warned you about your outbursts. Deputy Clerk, please escort Madame Folly out of my courtroom!

Madame Folly: Rolling her eyes, whatever…

Judge: Lady Wisdom, I apologize for that interruption. Defendant, ask your question again.

Defendant: Lady Wisdom, could you tell the court about the girl she met online?

Lady Wisdom: Yes, I would be glad to. She was dealing with an intense battle with Fear that night. She didn't want Fear in her life anymore, but she didn't know how to move forward without him. He was trying to pull her in his direction. They were in a tug-a-war match at that point. She was so exhausted.

So, I encouraged her to go into this Christian chat room. A place she had been visiting.

There was a girl in the chatroom named Amy who heard her cry for help through the words she texted and encouraged her to join her in a private chat room. She spoke with her for some time and led her back to Jesus. Fear no longer had her attention. She was free! It was so pleasant to see that grin back on her face, and the glow on her cheeks. A sense of relief washed over her as she eagerly invited peace, the Prince of Peace, back into her life. It showed on her face!

Amy didn't stop there. Oh no, they exchanged emails, and she gave her two homework assignments.
I was so proud of her. She was to read each chapter of Romans and then give a synopsis of each chapter after she finished reading them.
Amy wanted to help her get reacquainted with God. It was the beginning of a new chapter for her.

Defendant: Thank you, Lady Wisdom.

Judge: Plaintiff, do you want to cross?

Plaintiff: I rest.

Judge: Lady Wisdom, you may step down. We are going to take a half an hour break.

In the hallway

Fear: In an alarming voice to anyone who would listen: Has anyone been watching the news? The storm has returned! It's uh… worse than the first time. It's chaotic. I don't know why we are here still. It's the end of the world as we know it. Whatever those in authority tell you to do, do it. Your life depends on it. They know what they are doing.

Everyone started heading back into the courtroom.

Chapter 3

Discovery

"Then Peter and the other apostles answered and said, we ought to obey God rather than men."

Acts 5:29

Clerk: All rise. Court is now in session. Judge Justice is presiding.

Judge: Deputy Clerk, you may escort Madame Folly back into the courtroom. Thank you. You may take your seat. We call the Case of Mistaken Identity now in session.

Fear: Oh no, the storm, the storm, take cover. Go home where it is safe! It's going to kill us all!

Judge: This is not appropriate. Fear, be quiet or I will have you removed from the courtroom.

Fear:, shaking, standing like a reed in the wind: No, the storm is back and is going to kill us all!

Judge: Deputy Clerk, please escort Fear out of my courtroom! Does the Defendant have a witness they would like to call to the stand?

Defendant: Your Honor, I would like to call Faith to the stand.

Judge: Faith, please take the stand. Before you sit, can you please raise your right hand? Do you promise to tell the whole truth, nothing but the truth, so help you, God?

Faith: I do.

Judge: Thank you, Faith. You may take your seat.

Defendant: Faith, how did you come to know the young lady?
Faith: I came to know her as a child when she invited Jesus into her heart. She has always struggled with her walk with me.

Defendant: Now, before Fear was escorted out of the courtroom, he was speaking about a storm. Will you please address the court about this storm and how it affected people?

Faith: The storm caused quite a ruckus in the land. People didn't know what to believe. Fear was running rampant, and many followed him. There were people that stood against the protocol even while shaking in their boots. These individuals were cut from a different cloth. Just like how David stood up to Goliath, they stood up as well! They understood what was at stake but were determined to be free and be an example to others. Not in their own strength, of course. There was a bigger picture, and they were working with God to accomplish that! Their refusal to follow the protocol on the land caused shock, judgment, and shunning. This was an enemy like no other, for its desire was complete obedience, even if what they were being asked to do had no common sense to it.

Defendant: Can you tell the court how it affected her?

Faith: Well, before the storm started or any suggestion of the storm, she was getting ready to write. She had her schedule all lined up for her days of writing and knew this was her time. When the storm first came, it pained her to see the change across the land. At the same time of seeing this, her own house was going through a storm of its own. She wanted to write, but she was too angry at the injustice around her and the effect it was having on her house and the people. There was a darkness across the land that was felt.

She tried to tune out the surrounding battle by listening to music throughout the day and into the night. Nightmares troubled her sleep, so she never felt well rested. Sometimes she would fall asleep on the couch and awake in fright. She would read her Bible, trying so hard to stay focused on the words on the pages.

She picked up her pen and wrote in her journal what God shared with her. She was not ready to write professionally. Her writing would not have been pleasant to read because the words would have been angry. Now that I think about it, she had not journaled in at least a decade. Not long after that, she started drawing again, something she hadn't done in decades.

She didn't go out like she once did because of the protocol. God encouraged her to stand strong against the protocol for following Fear was not living. Because of her refusal to obey the protocol, she dealt with disdain. She was learning well, I must add, how to walk with me. She would often say, "I wish I was a bird. Birds are free!"

"For we walk by faith, not by sight." 2 Corinthians 5:7

Man did not make it easy for her, as she stepped out, she dealt with opposition. Fear was present, but she wasn't about to let him have the upper hand. Sometimes she did it shaking, sometimes in tears, sometimes she fell, but she got back up. She wasn't about to surrender to Fear.

It was not a comfortable time for anyone, but while the turbulence was going on around her, she was finding her place, her voice, her calling. It might have looked messy to onlookers, but she was finding her place again with the God of her youth, and now her calling was becoming crystal clear to her.

What you saw was what you got. She didn't realize that the underpinnings of her calling were being laid. Even though at the time it looked messy, for laying a foundation is messy, she found God in the storm's eye and in that she found her place beside Him, forever.

I have a truth I would like to share with the court- "Let us here the whole conclusion of the whole matter: fear God and keep his commandments: for this is the whole duty of man."
Ecclesiastes 12:13

Defendant: Thank You, Faith.

Judge: Faith, you may step down.

Defendant: Judge, I would like to take the stand and share with the court a bit of my now story.

Judge: That would be great, Sadie. Before you sit, can you please raise your right hand? Do you promise to tell the whole truth, nothing but the truth, so help you, God?

Defendant: Yes!

Defendant: Ladies and gentlemen, what you have heard are bits and pieces of my story. I have struggled all my life with my walk with God. The storm forced me into a fight-or-flight stance. I fought! During that time, I discovered my purpose and accepted it. God's promise to me - no one will rob you of your story. My place in this world is in his hands. Writing is only part of my story. I watch with eagerness as God unfolds the rest. Thank you. I rest in Jesus!

Judge: Does the defense have any more witnesses to call?

Defendant: No, Your Honor, the defense rests their case.

Judge: Does the prosecutor have any more witnesses to call?

Plaintiff: No, Your Honor, the prosecutor rests their case.

Madame Folly: Wait a minute, this is not everything!

Judge: This is all I need to hear, thank you. We will now hear closing statements. Plaintiff, you may give your closing statement.

Plaintiff: Thank you, Your Honor.
We have shown the courts her story, one filled with rebellious behavior, lack of respect towards authority.

Not to mention she does not measure up to God's standards.

She is not an ideal candidate for the calling God has for her. Your Honor, we ask for your verdict of guilty.

Judge: Thank you, Plaintiff. Do you want to reserve time for rebuttal?

Plaintiff: No, Your Honor.

Judge: Alright. Defense, you may give your closing statement now.

Defendant: Thank you, Your Honor. God has prepared me for my life's purpose. Jesus has redeemed my younger years. As far as being disobedient to authority during the storm, sometimes one must choose if it is better to obey men or God. I obeyed God's leading. I will not let others use my past to dictate my future. My story is God's story. I am asking for a verdict of not guilty. I leave the court with these three truths:

"There is therefore now no condemnation to them which are in Christ Jesus, who walk not after the flesh, but after the spirit." Romans 8:1

"Many are the afflictions of the righteous: but the LORD delivers him out of them all." Psalm 34:19

"For you see your calling, brethren, how that few wise men after the flesh, few mighty, few noble, are called: but God has chosen the foolish things of the world to confound the things which are mighty; and base things of the world, and things which are despised, hath God chosen, yea, and things which are not, to bring to the nought things that are: that no flesh should glory in his presence." 1 Corinthians 1:26- 29

Judge: The court will now be in recess while I deliberate.

Sometime later

Clerk: All rise.

Court is now in session. Honorable Judge Justice is presiding.

Judge: Thank you, you may take your seat.

We call the Case of Mistaken Identity now in session.
Sadie is found not guilty and freed from Condemnation due to a case of mistaken identity. Sadie is free from all the accusations made against her. The blood of Jesus and the word of her testimony have redeemed her. She is truly deserving of her calling. It was tailor made for her! It's her story! Case closed!

"Train up a child in the way they should go: and when he is old, he will not depart from it." Proverbs 22:6

Sadie, on her knees in tears, thanked God for his goodness while a victorious cheer erupted in the courtroom. She was now free to love her story. She felt a sigh of relief knowing that everything up to that point was behind her and now she was free to walk forward and be the voice God called her to be.

Sadie: Here I come, world!

"They have overcome by the blood of the lamb, and the word of their testimony." Revelation 12:11

A Case of Mistaken Identity

The court acquitted Sadie of all charges. Free of condemnation, free to love her story to the fullest!

Judge Justice

Chapter 4

Evidence

The evidence that was collected in the court case.

"What shall we then say to these things? If God be for us, who can be against us?" Romans 8:31

Submitted by Lady Wisdom
"but I say unto you, that ye resist not evil: but whosoever shall smite thee on thy right cheek, turn to him the other cheek." Matthew 5:39

Submitted by Lady Prudence
"They have overcome by the blood of the lamb, and the word of their testimony. " Revelation 12:11

Submitted by Lady Wisdom
"When I was a child, I spoke and thought and reasoned as a child. But when I grew up, I put away childish things." I Corinthians 13:11 (NLT)

Submitted by Sadie
"Do not be misled: Bad company corrupts good character."
I Corinthians 15:33 (NIV)

Submitted by Lady Prudence
"The LORD is nigh unto them that are of a broken heart; and seventh such as be of a contrite spirit." Psalm 34:18

Submitted by Madame Folly
"There is therefore now no condemnation to them which are in Christ Jesus, who **walk not after the flesh**, but after the Spirit." Romans 8:1 (emphasis by author)
She is guilty of condemnation.

FORGIVEN
Judge Justice
"for all have sinned and come short of the glory of God."
Romans 3:23-24

Submitted by Lady Prudence
"There is no fear in love, but perfect love casteth out fear: because fear has torment. He that feareth is not made perfect in love." I John 4:18 (emphasis by author)

Submitted by Lady Wisdom
"Let us hear the whole conclusion of the whole matter: fear God and keep his commandments: for this is the whole duty of man."
Ecclesiastes 12:13

Submitted by Faith
"Many are the afflictions of the righteous: but the LORD delivers him out of them all." Psalm 34:19

Submitted by Sadie
"For you see your calling, brethren, how that few wise men after the flesh, few mighty, few noble, are called: but God has chosen the foolish things of the world to confound the things which are mighty; and base things of the world, and things which are despised, hath God chosen, yea, and things which are not, to bring to the nought things that are: that no flesh should glory in his presence." 1 Corinthians. 1:26- 29

Time and time again, men have tried to infiltrate my story.

Conclusion

The story that you just read was a mock trial involving Sadie and Condemnation, with Judge Justice overseeing the case as the presiding judge. This mock trial is a fictional story with bits from my story. Sadie, a Hebrew name, means "finding one's place." With all my wanderings from such a young age, that was what I was searching for: "my place." We each have a story. What you do with the story God has given you is up to you. But know you are the only one that can fulfill it. For example, no two writers write the same. Don't let others dictate to you what your story is to be, therefore robbing you of what is yours! Seek God and find out what His story is for you. Then love your story to the fullest!

We each have a story. What you do with the story God has given you is up to you.

Obsessed with Success

As a young girl, I found fairy tales fascinating. I held a special affinity with *Snow White*. Her stepmother, the Queen, had a magical mirror she spoke with every morning. "Oh, magic mirror on the wall. Who is the fairest of them all?" Her preoccupation with how she fared in her position left no room for anyone else. One day, to her chagrin, the mirror mentioned another fairer than her, a young girl named Snow White. In fear, she summoned a huntsman and commanded him to locate Snow White and end her life. The huntsman didn't follow through with her orders, but warned Snow White of the Queen's evil intention. Snow White ran away to a cottage deep in the woods, inhabited by dwarves. When the wicked queen realized that the huntsman had betrayed her, she took matters into her own hands. She transformed herself into a little old lady, someone the Princess would trust, and cursed an apple. While the dwarves worked in the mines, she went to the quaint cottage with a gift for Snow White. Snow White answered the door, taken aback by the little old lady. However, she did not discern the danger before her. Snow White accepted the basket of apples the old lady offered her, and, with one bite of the cursed apple, she fell to the floor. The Queen, clearly a witch, cackled with delight as she thought she had finished Snow White's story. However, as she walked home, a furious storm came across the land, making it hard for her to see her way home. With one step, she fell off the cliff and ended her story. True love resuscitated Snow White and elevated her to her rightful position as queen of the land! This story reminded me of my mirror history research. Egyptians made a mirror by pressing metal and polishing it until there was a reflection. Or should I say a resemblance to one? So, the beauty of this story is the wicked Queen had just a part of Snow White's story. Her fixation on Snow White's story came at the expense of her own narrative!

"So are the ways of everyone that is greedy for gain; which takes away the life of the owners thereof."
Proverbs 1:19

God's Gift

The gift that costs God everything!

Admit you are a sinner, and you cannot save yourself.
"For by grace are ye saved through faith; and that not of yourselves: it is the gift of God: not of works, lest any man should boast."
Ephesians 2:8-9

Believe on Jesus, for the finished work on the cross. He paid the ultimate price for your salvation.
"For God so loved the world, that he gave his only begotten Son, that whosoever believeth in him should not perish, but have everlasting life."
John 3:16

Confess with your mouth and believe in your heart.
"That if thou shalt confess with thy mouth the Lord Jesus, and shalt believe in thine heart that God hath raised him from the dead, thou shalt be saved. For with the heart man believeth unto righteousness; and with the mouth confession is made unto salvation."
Romans 10:9-10

Prayer:
Lord Jesus, forgive me of my sins, and make your home in my heart and teach me how to walk in this new life.
In Jesus' name, amen.

Now, go tell someone what you did.

Welcome to the family of God!

If you accepted Jesus, let me know by sending me an email at lizzy@eowrites.com and I'll send you a free small New Testament Bible.

Acknowledgments

A shout out of thanks to Christian Book Academy and especially my pod ladies.

A sincere thank you to my husband Joel and my daughter Sarah, as I worked tirelessly to finish this story.

Thank you, Joy, for inspiring me to write a fictional story.

Last but not least, God for walking me through the process and giving me the idea of writing a story involving Proverbs.

About the Author

Lizzy has been married for 27 years. She and her husband enjoy traveling throughout the United States on their Harley-Davidson motorcycle.

Her passion is sharing God's love through her art and writing. She hopes to get *I Am Special*, and *Ancient Text* published in 2025.

"Never judge a book by its cover. What you find inside the pages might surprise you. "

Find out more about Lizzy at:
http://www.eowrites.com/

Blog: https://www.eowrites.com/

Linked In: https://www.linkedin.com/in/elizabetho/

Note from the Author:

"A word fitly spoken is like apples of gold in pictures of silver."
Proverbs 25:11

If you have enjoyed this book, would you consider reviewing it on Amazon.com? Thank you!